Koala Country

A Story of an Australian Eucalyptus Forest

by Deborah Dennard

Illustrated by James McKinnon

Soundprints
Where Children Discover...

For Jerry—D.D.

I would like to dedicate my work in this book to my wife, Sue, who possesses an inexhaustible supply of encouragement and praise and also to all the wild dwellers of the forest, the air, the sea, and the land; and to the idea that Humanity may evolve sufficiently to become a friend to them all—J.M.

Art direction: Diane Hinze Kanzler; Ashley Andersen
Book Layout: Scott Findlay; Shields & Partners, Westport, CT
Editor: Judy Gitenstein

First edition 2000
10 9 8 7 6 5 4 3 2 1
Printed in Belgium

Acknowledgments:
  Our thanks to Ann Sharp of the Australian Koala Foundation for her curatorial review.
  The author would like to give additional thanks to Deborah Tagart, Australian Koala Foundation; and Georgeanne Irvine, San Diego Zoo.

Library of Congress Cataloging-in-Publication Data

Dennard, Deborah.
    Koala Country: a story of an Australian eucalyptus forest / by Deborah Dennard; illustrated by James McKinnon. — 1st ed.
        p. cm.
    Summary: A mother koala and her joey feed and observe the other animal inhabitants of their fragile eucalyptus forest home.
    ISBN 1-56899-887-2 (hardcover) — ISBN 1-56899-888-0 (pbk.)
    1. Koala—Juvenile fiction. [1. Koala—Fiction. 2. Zoology—Australia—Fiction.] I. McKinnon, James, ill. II. Title.

PZ10.3.D386 Ko 2000
[Fic] — dc21
                                                                00-023166
                                                                CIP
                                                                AC

Koala Country

A Story of an Australian Eucalyptus Forest

by Deborah Dennard

Illustrated by James McKinnon

It is a clear afternoon in a eucalyptus forest in New South Wales, Australia. It is October—springtime in this part of the world. A mother koala straddles a branch high in a forest red gum tree while her baby, known as a joey, rides piggyback. He yawns deeply and settles down for more of his day-long rest, hidden well in the fragrant clusters of silver-green eucalyptus leaves that sway gently in the breeze. Birds are everywhere in the forest around the koalas.

Eastern rosellas chatter as they feed in the grasses below. Rainbow lorikeets are drawn to the fragrant yellow-white eucalyptus flowers. One pair of lorikeets explores a tree hollow for a nest site, as two superb fairy-wrens pop up from the underbrush. They perch on a low banksia branch. High, clear trills pour from their throats. The mother koala yawns deeply, and tries to ignore their noisy antics.

A thumping noise vibrates from the ground below. It comes from a family of red-necked wallabies. Using their tails for balance, they hop from a gully nearby. A baby wallaby pokes his head into his mother's pouch for a quick sip of milk. A much smaller baby peers from another mother's pouch. Soon all of the wallabies settle down to enjoy the lovely spring afternoon. From her high, safe gum tree branch, the mother koala pays no mind to the wallabies far below.

The mother koala opens her eyes and reaches for a eucalyptus twig with the two thumbs and three fingers of one hand. She sniffs the leaves carefully. Some are poisonous and some she will be able to digest easily. The smell is not quite right, so she pushes these leaves away then pulls another branch closer. She selects leaves that suit her, snips them off with her sharp front teeth, then chews slowly with her back teeth. Soon the mother koala naps again.

A rainbow bee-eater emerges from his tunnel nest deep in the side of the gully. With twists, turns, and nearly impossible-to-do swoops, he catches flying insects. In moments he has his fill and returns to his tunnel nest to feed hungry babies waiting inside. As his mother naps, the joey watches the acrobatic bird, then climbs to the top of his mother's head. She grunts her displeasure, but lets him remain.

Closer to the koalas' tree, an echidna scuttles into view. At the end of his snout, a long, thin, sticky tongue darts out of a slit-like mouth in search of ants and termites. Not far away, the grass parts and a huge, hungry carpet python slithers powerfully into view. The mother koala awakens and eyes the reptile who could so easily take her baby if she were careless. Her best defense is to sit perfectly still, while the animals around her move to protect themselves.

A warning thump scatters the wallabies at top speed. The parrots fly away with a squawk. The echidna digs forcefully. Within seconds he is half buried, with only his sharp spines showing. The carpet python does not care. Swiftly, silently, a bush rat becomes his meal, and the snake slithers away to digest his feast in peace.

From the safety of his high perch, the joey is restless from all of the excitement below. Once the danger has passed, he cuddles with his mother for security.

All is quiet until dusk. As darkness descends, the koalas awake to the sound of a roaring, snoring bellow. It is the call of a male koala.

It is now mating time. Male koalas make a commotion to proclaim their territories and to make other koalas aware of their presence. One koala in a tree across the gully points his head to the sky and roars. He grasps the tree with both hands and rubs the scent gland on his chest up and down. The smell he leaves behind will let other koalas know he has been there.

Fully awake now, the mother koala spots tempting leaves on another gum tree. Bottom first, she carefully climbs down the tree, her baby holding tight. She walks awkwardly across the ground. Using her arms to pull and her legs to push, she easily scales the new tree. Seconds later, a large shadow swoops through the night and lands in the tree above the koalas. It is a flying fox. Upside down, it feeds on eucalyptus blossoms for nectar and pollen as the koalas feed on leaves. The tree provides food for both bat and koala as well as many other mammals, birds, and insects.

From a nest made of leaves shaped into a hollow ball, a ring-tailed possum with babies clinging to her back emerges. She wraps her tail around branches for balance and climbs past the koalas in her search for leaves and fruit.

But the koala mother seems not to care. Instead, she watches two male koalas in another gum tree. One is smaller and younger than the other. They growl, bellow, and tug at each other's ears as a contest to see who is stronger. The older koala lashes out with his long arms and claws, barely missing the younger koala's face. The younger male snorts and backs away. Today he will not win the battle. Someday that may change.

The joey stirs, then slowly climbs from his mother's back. This is the first time he has been strong and brave enough to leave the warm, safe touch of his mother. He cautiously tries a few tender leaves, surveying the tree and the night with eyes of growing independence.

The koala mother looks at her growing baby. Soon she will mate again and a new, tiny joey no bigger than a bumblebee will make its way into the safety of her pouch. When that time comes, the older joey will be ready to live on his own. He may stay nearby for a while, but his mother will not notice. She will be too busy with the new life in her pouch, with naps to take and leaves to eat.

Before the faintest hints of morning begin to brighten the sky, before the laughing kookaburras herald the dawn with their cackling calls, the koala and her joey are together again. They cuddle and prepare for another day's rest. For now, all is as it should be in their fragile eucalyptus forest home.

NEW SOUTH WALES, AUSTRALIA

When Europeans first settled Australia in the late 1700s, much of the
eastern coast of the continent was covered by eucalyptus forests. Since
then, roughly 80 percent of the eucalyptus forests where koalas lived has
been logged, cleared for crops or pastureland, or has been developed into
towns or cities. Today koalas are found in the wild in New South Wales,
as well as in Queensland, Victoria, and South Australia.

About an Australian Eucalyptus Forest

When people think of Australia, they think of koalas. Most Australians have never actually seen a koala in the wild. When people think of koalas, they think of adorable, almost teddy bear-like animals, yet koalas are in real danger today. Between 1870 and 1927, millions of koalas were killed for their fur. For koalas to survive, their forest homes must be saved, and more must be understood about these gentle animals.

Koalas look like bears but they are marsupials and have pouches for rearing young just like kangaroos. Newborn joeys must find their way into the pouch. After six months in the pouch drinking milk, koalas are about eight inches long. They leave the pouch and spend six months riding on their mother's back. Mother koalas and their babies call to each other with soft grunts. If a mother koala senses danger, she calls her baby to return to a safer place.

Many mysteries surround koalas. The eucalyptus leaves they eat are poisonous to most animals, yet koalas are able to digest many of them safely. Koalas can tell by their smell which leaves are safe and which are not. Eucalyptus forests take a long time to regrow once they have been cleared, and koalas are very picky about their trees. They choose certain trees and leaves, and ignore others. When confronted by a predator, often the domestic dog, they will scratch and bite to defend themselves if cornered, and try to reach the safety of the nearest tree. Often, though, koalas are easily killed.

Koalas do not adapt well to change and are totally dependent on eucalyptus forests for food, water, shelter, and contact with other koalas. Not until people understand the importance of eucalyptus trees to koalas, and take steps to protect those trees, will these creatures have a chance for survival.

To learn more about koala conservation contact the Australian Koala Foundation at: www.savethekoala.com.

Glossary

▲ *Koala*

▲ *Forest red gum*

▲ *Magpie*

▲ *Red-necked wallaby*

▲ *Rainbow bee-eater*

▲ *Echidna*

▲ *Grass tree*

▲ *Eastern rosellas*

▲ *Laughing kookaburras*